THE GRAB-BAG PARTY

By Betsy Maestro

Illustrated by Giulio Maestro

A GOLDEN BOOK • NEW YORK

Western Publishing Company, Inc., Racine, Wisconsin 53404

"Isn't spring great!" said Cat. "Let's have a party, a spring celebration."

"Good idea!" said Mouse, sipping his tea.

Just then the gate opened and Snake slithered in.

"This weather is wonderful," Snake said. "I think we should have a party."

"We think so, too," said Cat. "How about a grab-bag party tomorrow at my house?"

"Perfect!" said Mouse.

"Let's invite Duck, Bear, and Frog," suggested Cat. All the friends agreed.

Later that day, they each went to the store to buy a grab-bag gift.

Cat found the perfect gift—a fancy pair of sunglasses. "Just the thing for lying around in the sun," she said.

Snake picked out a scarf. "Someone is going to be lucky to get this!" she said as she tried it on.

Mouse chose an umbrella.
"No one likes to get wet," he
said. "Fur does get so soggy!"

Duck spotted a shiny
black diving mask. "Just what
I was looking for!" she
exclaimed.

Frog headed for the swimwear department. "Swimming weather is coming," he said, and he bought a bright red swimsuit.

And Bear chose a pair of sneakers. "Everyone likes to exercise," he said.

Early the next morning, the friends were busy preparing for the party. Snake and Duck blew up balloons. Cat made a chocolate cake. Bear picked flowers and put them in vases. Mouse and Frog went to the store to buy paper plates and punch. At last everything was ready.

That afternoon, they all arrived at Cat's house
dressed in their nicest clothes.
"Welcome to the grab-bag party," said Cat.
The friends put their gifts into a big box. Then they
played hide-and-seek and ate the chocolate cake.

When it was time for the grab-bag, everyone was excited. They took turns reaching into the box.

Duck went first. She pulled out a long package and unwrapped it. "An umbrella! I've never had one of these before," she said.

It was Snake's turn next. "My first pair of sneakers!" she said as she opened her gift.

Then Mouse picked a package. "Oh, my," he said. "I've never had such a long scarf."

Frog got the sunglasses. "I can't wait to wear them," he said.

Finally, Bear and Cat reached into the box. When Bear saw the diving mask, he was surprised. "What an interesting gift," he said.

Cat unwrapped the swimsuit. "It's lovely," she said.

The friends thanked each other for their presents. Then it was time to go home.

The next day it rained. Duck went outside to try her new umbrella. "This really keeps me dry," she thought, "but I'd rather be wet!"

So Duck let the umbrella fill with water.

But when she stepped in. the umbrella tipped over and the water ran out. "I'd better stick to the pond," Duck said.

Meanwhile, Mouse was trying on his new scarf. The ends dragged on the floor, so he wrapped the scarf around a few more times. But when he tried to walk, he fell down. He couldn't get up!

He began to roll. At last the scarf unwound, and he was free.

"I think this scarf is a little long for me," Mouse said sadly.

Snake was at home, too, trying on her new sneakers. She slithered into one. "It's so dark," she said. "This can't be right." So she got in backwards. "Now I can see!"

She tried to move across the floor, but the sneaker stood still.

"I guess I can't wear sneakers," Snake said glumly.

The rain stopped and the sun came out. Bear, Cat, and Frog hurried to the pond with their gifts.

Bear tried fitting his diving mask over one eye, then he tried it on his nose. But the mask was too small. "Oh, well," he sighed. "I never liked diving anyway."

Cat had put on her new swimsuit. She put one foot into the water. It felt cold and wet. She didn't like it at all. "I'm not really much of a swimmer," Cat said. "In fact, I hate the water!"

Frog was wearing his new sunglasses, even though they were too big. Suddenly he saw a fat bug swim by. *Splash!* He dove into the water. When Frog came up, the sunglasses were no longer on his nose. And the bug had gotten away!

"I guess sunglasses are not for me," he said.

Mouse, Duck, and Snake stood on the shore, watching.

"I see we're all having trouble," said Mouse.

"Maybe we got the wrong presents," said Duck.

"We could return them to the store," said Snake.

"I have a better idea," said Frog, coming out of the water. "Let's have a swapping party."

So later on, the friends met at Snake's house. They put their gifts on a table. Then they each picked the gift they wanted.

The next morning, all six friends were enjoying their new gifts.

Cat's sunglasses fit her perfectly.

Snake paraded around in her scarf.

Even though it was sunny, Mouse was using his umbrella. "My fur will never be soggy again!" he exclaimed.

Bear came jogging by in his sneakers.
Duck was diving into the pond. "This mask is great!"
she shouted. "Now I can see underwater."
Nearby, Frog was splashing around in his swimsuit.

Later, they all met for tea.
"I guess everything worked out," said Cat.
"Yes," said Mouse. "Now everyone's happy."
"That's true," said Frog. "But the best part is that we got to have two parties instead of one!"
And everyone agreed.